Amazing Daddy

Rachel Bright

ORCHARD

My daddy is a **hundred** things,
A hundred things and **more!**

He's all the things
that you would think

a BRILLIANT dad is for.

He's big and kind and hairy.
He smells of safe and warm.

I love him from his top to toe,
From dusk right through to dawn.

I love
his morning
grumpy face...

. . . and his happy smile.

I love it when we
stay in bed to
Snuggle up a while.

And when we're making breakfast,
If Daddy is in charge,
Whatever we are having . . .

When he has to go to work,
I miss him not at home.
So, just in case he's
missing me . . .

Often on the weekends,
he's busy in the shed.

He's got a lot of GOOD iDEAS
inside his daddy head!

And even when I'm naughty,
he doesn't get upset.

He just makes me think about it . . .

. . . on the
naughty
person
step.

I love it when we
play all day
in scrambles, rolls and climbs.

And if I'm getting tired,
he will carry
me sometimes.

Yes, I'd like to be like Daddy when I'm **big** and **old** one day.

But the oldness that
my daddy has is
VERY
far away.

My **favourite** thing is bedtime,
when we **bundle** in a heap.

He'll tuck me in
and read to me . . .

...until I fall asleep.

Some nights, if I'm lucky,
he'll doze off in my chair,

And even though
he snores quite
LOUD

I'd rather he was there.

Yes, my daddy is AMAZING for a thousand different reasons.

He's a year-round SUPERHERO,

a daddy for all seasons!

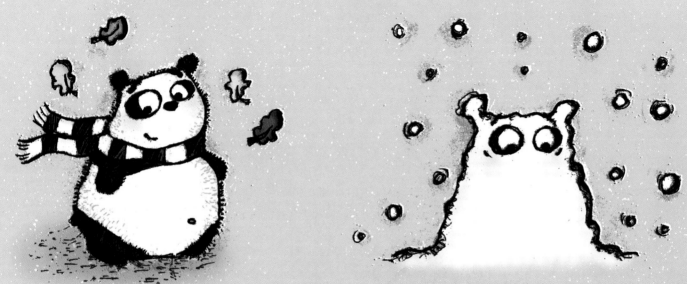

But, Daddy, it's not Only

the hundred things you DO...

. . . that make you so AMAZING,

That make you just so
YOU!
It's all the days of you and me,
The Daddy times so far . . .

Daddy, this **am^aZi**n**gn**e**SS**, it's simply . . .

. . . who

you

are.